LEVEL 2 READER

My Magical Friends

Baby Dragon Takes Flight

W9-BDN-166

by Jessica Lee Anderson
illustrated by Wendy Tan

SCHOLASTIC INC.

For Ava and Olive and their magical friendship.
—J.L.A.

To Lucky, my magical puppy!
—Wendy Tan Shiau Wei

ISBN 978-1-338-89082-2

10 9 8 7 6 5 4 3 2 1   23 24 25 26 27

Printed in China   68
First edition 2023
Original book design by Joan Moloney

Shelby went over to her best friend
Isabella's house.
"Come on," said Isabella. "There is a surprise
in my tree house."
"But first, let's put on our crowns," said Shelby.
When the girls played together, they loved
to look like princesses.

Shelby climbed up the ladder to the tree house.
Isabella followed her.
"Wow! My play set is here," said Shelby.
"Surprise! Your grandma brought it here,"
said Isabella.

You know what would make this day better? The magic bracelet!" said Shelby.

Shelby pulled out a small gold box with a magic bracelet inside.

Whenever Shelby wore it, the girls traveled to a magic forest.

Once they even met a winged horse!

The bracelet glowed when Shelby put it on.
Isabella and Shelby grabbed hands and looked
at the bracelet.
They felt a funny tug and a tingle.
There was a flash of light.

The girls blinked as they looked around.
They were not in Isabella's tree house anymore.
They were standing in a magical tree house!
It glowed with lights and sparkles.
"Your magic bracelet worked again!" exclaimed
Isabella.

The girls peeked out the window.

They could see the castle in the distance.

"Help!" yelled a voice from the forest.

"Did you hear that?" asked Shelby.

"Yes, let's find out what's wrong," said Isabella.

"But how do we get down?" asked Shelby. The magical tree house was high up. They did not see a ladder.

"We can use the gold vines to climb down," said Isabella.

"Good idea," said Shelby.

Isabella grabbed a gold vine.

So did Shelby.

They carefully climbed down the tree.

"We did it!" said Isabella.

When they got to the ground, it was hard to tell which way to go.

"Help!" yelled the voice again.

The girls followed the sound of the voice.

Finally, the voice led them to a tall oak.
They looked up and saw something moving.
It had shiny blue scales and its wings looked
like leather.

"It's a baby dragon!" exclaimed Shelby.

"My name is Lyla," said the dragon, "and I'm stuck up here!"

"We can help you, Lyla," said Shelby. "We are Princesses Shelby and Isabella."

Shelby winked at Isabella.

"What happened?" asked Isabella.

"Today was my first flying lesson," said Lyla, "and I crashed into this tree."

"Are you hurt?" asked Shelby.

"No, but I am scared I might make another mistake," said Lyla.

Shelby thought of what her grandma always said.
"My grandma says we can learn from our mistakes," said Shelby.
"Things get easier with practice," said Isabella.

"Try to climb down slowly and carefully," said Isabella.

"That's how we climbed down from the tree house," said Shelby.

Lyla backed her way off the branch.

The branch bounced. The silver leaves in the tree shook.

"I am too scared to come down," said Lyla.

Keep trying, Lyla," said Isabella.

You got this!" cheered Shelby.

You princesses believe in me?" Lyla asked.

Yes!" the girls said. They gave the baby dragon

two thumbs-up.

Lyla climbed part of the way down the tree.
She missed a branch and stumbled.
"Uh-oh," the girls said.
They worried the baby dragon might fall.

"Maybe flying down would be safer," said Isabella.

"Flying might seem scary now, but it will get easier with practice," said Shelby.

Lyla flapped her wings.

"Keep going. You're almost there, Lyla," said Isabella.

Lyla flapped her wings harder.
She lifted into the air.
"You're flying!" cheered Shelby.

Lyla kept flapping her wings.
She flew the rest of the way out of the tree
and landed in Shelby's arms!
Isabella clapped.
"Way to go!" cheered Isabella.

Lyla looked at Shelby gratefully.
Isabella pulled a silver leaf off Lyla's wing.
"Thank you, Princesses!" said Lyla.

"Lyla! Where are you?" a voice called from the air.
"Over here, Aunt Sienna!" Lyla called.
Shelby and Isabella watched as a grand dragon
swooped down toward them.
"My aunt was teaching me how to fly before I
crashed," said Lyla.

"Aunt Sienna, I got stuck in a tree, but these princesses helped me," said Lyla.
"Thank you, Princesses! You will always be welcome in the enchanted forest," said Aunt Sienna.
Aunt Sienna bowed down to the girls in gratitude.
"That means a lot to us," said Shelby.

"I feel brave now thanks to these princesses," said Lyla.

"I am glad you are okay, Lyla. You *are* brave," Aunt Sienna said.

The dragons nuzzled their heads together.

"I think that is some sort of dragon hug," said Isabella.

"Magical," whispered Shelby.

The sun began to set.

Lyla yawned.

"It's getting late," said Aunt Sienna. "I can fly you princesses home if you show me the way."

"Wow!" said the girls.
In a flash, they flew toward
the magical tree house.

Lyla flew right next to
them all on her own!

Back at the magical tree house, the girls waved good-bye.

"Good-bye!" said the dragons.

Isabella and Shelby felt tired but happy.

It was time to go home.

Shelby and Isabella held hands and looked down at the magic bracelet.
The bracelet glowed. They felt a funny tug and a tingle.
Then they saw a flash of light.
Just like that, they were back in Isabella's tree house.

Shelby looked at her bracelet again.

"Check out this sparkly dragon charm!" said Shelby.

"That's amazing!" said Isabella.

When Isabella reached into her pocket, she found a silver leaf.

"Wow! Look at this, Shelby," said Isabella.

"Beautiful," said Shelby.

"This was the most magical adventure ever!"
said Isabella.

"I agree! The day has been full of surprises,"
said Shelby.

The girls spent the rest of the afternoon
playing and dreaming up their next adventure.